The FurFins

If you tiptoe to the seashore
and gaze out at the sea,
you might just spot a sparkly tail
or a friendly furry face.
You've just seen a FurFin and found
a very special place.

Shhh, FurFins are real . . .

The FurFins

CherryTail and the Mermaid Wedding

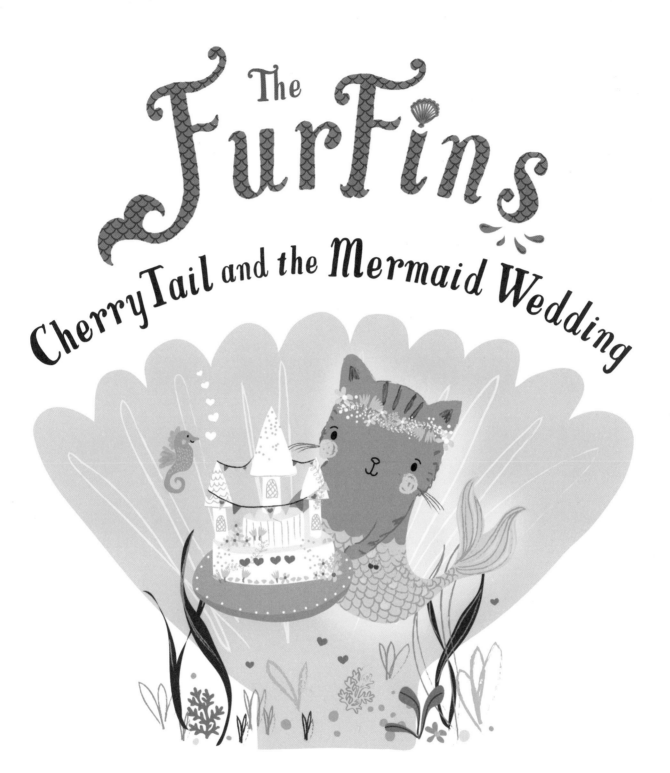

Written by
ALISON RITCHIE

Illustrated by
ALESS BAYLIS

BLOOMSBURY
CHILDREN'S BOOKS
LONDON OXFORD NEW YORK NEW DELHI SYDNEY

Deep beneath the silvery waves,
nestled in a kaleidoscope of colourful coral,
lies the magnificent Kingdom of Coralia.
This is where the FurFins live.

Look – there's StarTail and PosyTail, and over
there by the shimmering seaweed, that's TinyTail.

I wonder what they're
doing today?

StarTail was busy making beautiful headdresses, helped by her seahorse Shine.

"I'm so excited," she said. "I can't believe that Princess Coral is getting married today and we are going to be her bridesmaids!"

PosyTail and her seahorse Sparkle
were making pretty posies
for the wedding.

TinyTail and her seahorse Boo were
gathering sparkling sea confetti.

"It's going to be the best day
EVER," said TinyTail.
"But there's still so
much to do!"

Meanwhile at her café, CherryTail was busy making
the royal wedding cake. She was the best baker in the whole
of Coralia and her latest creation was magnificent.

It glistened with silver shells, sugar hearts and sparkles. "Ta-da!" CherryTail stepped back to show her seahorse Yum her handiwork. "A cake fit for a princess! I can't wait to show the others."

StarTail and TinyTail were already on their way.
They chatted happily as they headed for CherryTail's café.

"I bet the princess's cake will look AMAZING!" said TinyTail.

But when they arrived at the café, poor CherryTail was in tears. "The cake has DISAPPEARED," she cried. "I left it here while I was tidying up, and when I turned around again it had vanished!"

"Jumping jellyfish!" said StarTail. "Where could it have gone?"

"Don't worry, CherryTail," said TinyTail. "We'll find it. Let's go and see Cariad. She always knows how to help."

Cariad was a great big hug of an octopus, and when she saw
the FurFins' gloomy faces, she gave them all a big octo-cuddle.
"Oh deary me," she said. "Why so glum on this happy day, my lovelies?"

CherryTail sobbed. "The princess's wedding cake has been STOLEN! Who would do such a thing?"

"Well," said Cariad wisely, "if people are feeling sad, they sometimes do things that they don't really mean to do."

"Who'd be feeling sad on such a special day?" wondered TinyTail. "Maybe we can help them."

"And then we might find the cake too," added StarTail. "Come on, let's go!"

With no time to lose, CherryTail dried her tears and the three friends whooshed off in a whirl of bubbles. They searched the Kelp Forest . . .

and the Sandy Seabed, but everyone was happy and excited about Princess Coral's wedding.

"It's no use," sighed CherryTail. "We'll never get the cake back. The royal wedding is ruined and it's all my fault!"

But just then, they heard a gentle sobbing . . .

They followed the sound all the way to Ocean Bay where
they found WishTail, sitting all alone in the playground.

She was crying her eyes out,
and not even her seahorse Bubble
could comfort her.

"What's the matter, WishTail?"
TinyTail asked gently.

"It's my birthday today," WishTail cried.
"Everyone has forgotten because of the royal wedding."

"I wanted a birthday cake so badly, and when I saw the wedding cake in the café, I took it before I knew what I was doing . . .

But it didn't make me feel better at all.
I should never have taken it.
I'm sorry!"

And she started crying
all over again.

"Don't cry, WishTail," said StarTail.
"There's still time to put it right."

"Come on, we'll help you!"
said CherryTail.

With a flick of their tails, the FurFins swam off to deliver the cake to the palace, and then hurried back to TinyTail's pod to get ready for the wedding!

Full of excitement, the FurFins put on their special flowery headdresses and each of them chose a pretty heart-shaped necklace. But just as they were about to leave, CherryTail looked thoughtful.

"There's something I need to do," she said.
"I'll meet you at the palace."

"OK, but don't be too long," said TinyTail. "We can't be late!"

Back at her café, CherryTail whisked, baked and iced
quicker than she had ever done before.

"All done, Yum," she said.
"Now let's get to the wedding!"

And what a wedding it was!
Princess Coral looked beautiful in her
shining lace dress, and holding up the long,
shimmering train were the chief bridesmaids . . .

CherryTail,

PosyTail,

TinyTail

StarTail,

and WishTail!

The happy couple could not stop smiling.
Soon it was time to head off for the wedding feast.

First of all, CherryTail had
a very special surprise
for WishTail . . .

her very own
birthday cake!

"Thank you all for sharing this special day," Princess Coral said.
"It's someone else's special day too and we have an important song to sing!"

All the wedding guests sang HAPPY BIRTHDAY
as WishTail blew out her candles and made a wish.

"This is the best birthday EVER!"
she said. "Thank you, so much!"

Once everyone had enjoyed the delicious
cakes, they all gathered to wave the prince
and princess off on their honeymoon.

It was the perfect wedding day!
Fireworks popped and sparkled and everyone
celebrated into the night.

Then with a swish of their tails, the FurFins

set off together on another exciting adventure.

For Poppy – A.R.

For Lola – A.B.

BLOOMSBURY CHILDREN'S BOOKS
Bloomsbury Publishing Plc
50 Bedford Square, London, WC1B 3DP, UK

BLOOMSBURY, BLOOMSBURY CHILDREN'S BOOKS and the Diana logo are trademarks of Bloomsbury Publishing Plc

First published in Great Britain 2020 by Bloomsbury Publishing Plc
Text copyright © Bloomsbury Publishing Plc, 2020
Illustrations copyright © Aless Baylis, 2020

Aless Baylis has asserted her right under the Copyright, Designs and Patents Act, 1988, to be identified as Illustrator of this work

A catalogue record for this book is available from the British Library

ISBN: 978-1-5266-0657-0 (paperback)

2 4 6 8 10 9 7 5 3 1

Printed and bound in China by Leo Paper Products, Heshan, Guangdong
All papers used by Bloomsbury Publishing Plc are natural, recyclable products from wood grown in well managed forests.
The manufacturing processes conform to the environmental regulations of the country of origin

To find out more about our authors and books visit www.bloomsbury.com and sign up for our newsletters

See you again soon!

The End